Dora Saves MERMAID KINGDOM!

adapted by Michael Teitelbaum
based on the original teleplay by Valerie Walsh
illustrated by Artful Doodlers

Simon and Schuster/Nickelodeon

Based on the TV series *Dora the Explorer* as seen on Nick Jr.

Simon and Schuster
First published in Great Britain in 2007 by Simon & Schuster UK Ltd
Africa House, 64-78 Kingsway, London WC2B 6AH
A CBS Company
Originally published in the USA in 2007 by Simon Spotlight,
an imprint of Simon & Schuster Children's Division, New York.
© 2007 Viacom International Inc. All rights reserved.
NICKELODEON, Nick Jr., Dora the Explorer, and all related titles, logos and characters are
trademarks of Viacom International Inc.
All rights reserved including the right of reproduction in whole or in part in any form.
A CIP catalogue record for this book is available from the British Library
ISBN-13: 978-1-84738-155-2
Printed in Italy
10 9 8 7 6 5 4 3 2 1
Visit our websites: www.simonsays.co.uk
www.nick.co.uk

¡Hola! I'm Dora, and this is my best friend, Boots. We love the beach. We love the ocean, the warm sand, the bright blue sky, and the sunny sun.

Today is Clean-Up-the-Beach Day! That's when we make sure the beach is nice and clean!

Let's pick up all the rubbish and put it in the rubbish bag. Can you see any rubbish on the beach? *¡Sí!* There's a juice box! And there's a food wrapper!

¿*Qué más?* What else can you see? If you see more rubbish, say "*¡Basura!*"

¡Mira! There is a big clam on the beach. To tell the big clam to open, say *"¡Abre!"*

Great job! This big clam has
a special story to tell us.

The clam's story is about the Mermaid Kingdom.

Once upon a time a mean octopus dumped rubbish all over the Mermaid Kingdom. Luckily, a mermaid named Mariana found a magic crown so she could wish all the rubbish away. But a wave washed away Mariana's magic crown, and now she can't stop the mean octopus!

We need to help Mariana and the Mermaid Kingdom by finding that magic crown. Where could it be?

If you see the crown, say *"¡Corona!"* Can you see the magic crown? There it is!

Now we can bring the crown back to Mariana! Let's find the Mermaid Kingdom! Who do we ask for help when we don't know which way to go?

¡Sí! Map! Say "Map!"

Map says that we have to cross the Seashell Bridge and then go through Pirate Island to get to the Silly Sea. That's where we will find the Mermaid Kingdom. Come on! *¡Vámonos!*

We made it to the Seashell Bridge, but we can't get across!
That mean octopus has covered the bridge with rubbish.
    Let's look inside Backpack for something to clean up the
bridge. Say "Backpack!"

Is there anything in Backpack that we can use to clean up the bridge?

¡Si! A vacuum cleaner!

Now that we cleaned Seashell Bridge, we can get across. Let's count the shells as we cross. *Uno, dos, tres, cuatro, cinco, seis.* One, two, three, four, five, six.

¡Gracias! Thanks for helping us cross the bridge.

We made it to Pirate Island, but the Coconut Trees are in our way.

The Pirate Piggies show us how to do the Coconut Conga to get past the trees. Ready?
Wiggle, wiggle, wiggle!

Now we need to cross the Silly Sea. Look at all these Silly Sea animals. Who can help us swim past them all and through the Silly Sea? Yeah, dolphins!

My cousin Diego can help us call the dolphins.
To help Diego call the dolphins, we need to say "Squeak, squeak!"

We made it to the Mermaid Kingdom! Let's give Mariana back her magic crown so she can clean up the Mermaid Kingdom.

Oh, no! We're too late! The octopus threw a big net over Mariana. Now she's trapped!

Ooooh! Mariana gave me the crown just in time! I put it on, and now I'm a mermaid! *¡Fantástico!*

The magic crown lets me have one wish. What should we wish for?

Let's wish to clean up the Mermaid Kingdom. Ready? I wish to clean up the Mermaid Kingdom!

There is still rubbish in the kingdom! We're going to need help from our ocean friends!

Say "Clean-up time!"

¡Excelente! Mermaid Kingdom is getting clean.

Now we have to rescue Mariana. *¡Vámonos!*
Let's pull the net off of Mariana. *¡Muy bien!* Now she is free!

¡Mira! The net fell on the octopus, and he has fallen in the rubbish.

The octopus promises to put all rubbish in the rubbish dump from now on, instead of on the Mermaid Kingdom! Hooray! *¡Lo hicimos!* We did it!

Mariana needs her crown back, but she gave me a magical mermaid necklace so I can visit her anytime.

I know that we'll be friends forever, just like you and me! Thanks for helping me save Mariana and the Mermaid Kingdom! I couldn't have done it without you.